GIRAFFE GOES TO THE DOCTOR

Written by Sue Graves

Illustrated by Trevor Dunton

W
FRANKLIN WATTS
LONDON•SYDNEY

Giraffe was not feeling very well. His throat was **very sore**. He **didn't want to go to school** at all. He didn't even want to play with his little brother, and he always liked playing with him.

Mum said she was going to take Giraffe to see the doctor. She said Dr Sloth would soon make him better. But Giraffe said he **didn't want to go** to the doctor. He said he wanted the pink medicine that Mum always gave him when he wasn't well.

But Mum said Giraffe had a really sore throat.
She said he might have an **infection**. She said
the pink medicine wouldn't help this time.

Giraffe was **worried**. What if Dr Sloth was **scary**? What if she gave him **horrid medicine**? Giraffe was unhappy.

Just then, Grandpa came in. Giraffe told
Grandpa about his sore throat. He told him
that Mum was taking him to see the doctor.
Grandpa said that was **a good idea**.

Grandpa said that when he was a little giraffe, he fell and hurt his knee. His mum took him to see the doctor. He didn't want to go either. But the doctor was **very kind**. He put a big bandage on his knee. He gave Grandpa a sticker for **being brave**, too.

Best of all, Grandpa's friends wrote their names on his bandage. Grandpa said he was sad to take it off when his knee was better! Giraffe felt a **bit happier**.

That afternoon, Mum took Giraffe to see Dr Sloth.
Mum and Giraffe had to wait a **long time**,
so Giraffe played with a toy while he waited.
It was **good fun**.

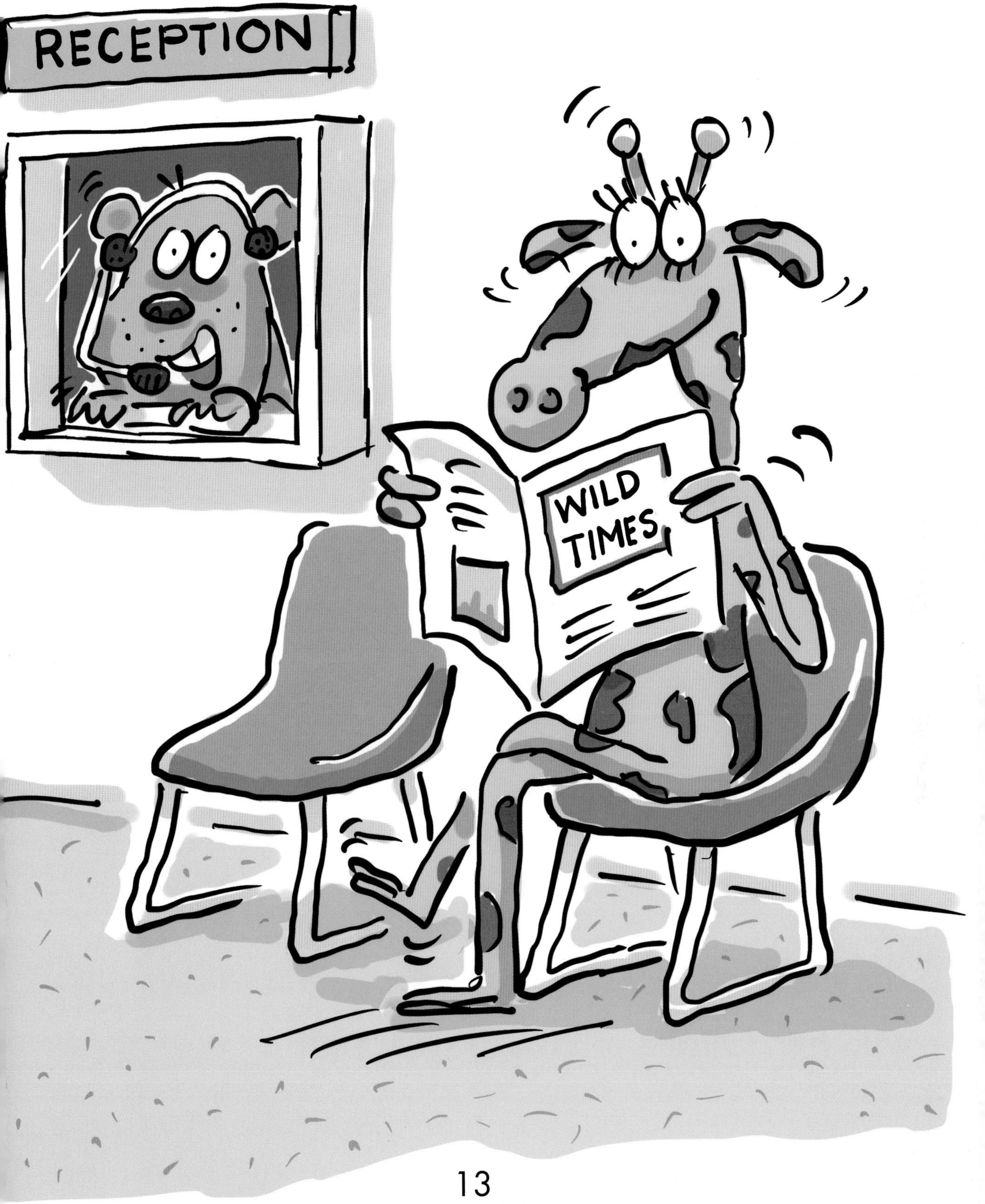
RECEPTION
WILD TIMES

Then Giraffe looked at a book Mum had brought with her. Giraffe felt **much happier**.

Soon, it was Giraffe's turn to see Dr Sloth.

Dr Sloth **wasn't scary** at all.

She smiled at Giraffe. She said he would soon be **feeling better**.

First of all, Dr Sloth took Giraffe's temperature.

Then Giraffe had to **stick out his tongue** and say "Ahh!". Dr Sloth **looked carefully** at Giraffe's sore throat.

Next, Dr Sloth looked in Giraffe's ears. It was **very tickly**.

Then Dr Sloth listened to Giraffe's chest.
She said it was sounding **very good**.

She even let Giraffe listen to his chest, too.
Giraffe was **really pleased**.

Dr Sloth said Giraffe had a throat infection. She said she would give him some **special medicine** to make it better.

Giraffe was worried that it wouldn't taste nice. But Dr Sloth said her medicines **always tasted nice**. Giraffe felt happier.

Dr Sloth told Giraffe he had to **stay in bed** until his sore throat was better. She said he couldn't go to school until then. She said she didn't want his friends to get sore throats, too.

Giraffe **was sad** not to see his friends.
But Dr Sloth gave him a **big sticker** to say
how **brave** he was. Giraffe felt **much happier**.

At home, Mum tucked Giraffe into bed.
She gave him his medicine. It **didn't taste horrid** at all. It tasted quite nice!
Giraffe was pleased.

Grandpa gave him some big juicy grapes to eat. They were delicious.

Dad made him a hot drink with honey in it. It made his throat feel much better.

Soon, Giraffe's sore throat was better.
Mum said he could get up. Giraffe was **glad**
he **felt better**. He said he was glad that
he went to see the doctor because it's **much**
nicer to feel well than ill!

A note about sharing this book

The *Experiences Matter* series has been developed to provide a starting point for further discussion on how children might deal with new experiences. It provides opportunities to explore ways of developing coping strategies as they face new challenges.
The series is set in the jungle with animal characters reflecting typical behaviour traits and attitudes often seen in young children.

Giraffe Goes to the Doctor
This story looks at some of the usual worries that children experience when they are ill.
It looks specifically at what might worry them when visiting the doctor and prepares them for what they might experience there.

How to use the book
The book is designed for adults to share with either an individual child, or a group of children, and as a starting point for discussion.

The book also provides visual support and repeated words and phrases to build reading confidence.

Before reading the story
Choose a time to read when you and the children are relaxed and have time to share the story.

Spend time looking at the illustrations and talk about what the book might be about before reading it together.

Encourage children to employ a phonics first approach to tackling new words by sounding the words out.

After reading, talk about the book with the children:

- After reading the book together, ask the children to retell the story in their own words.

- Invite the children to talk about their own experiences of being ill. What was the matter with them? Did they have to visit the doctor? Did they have to take special medicine? What was the surgery like? Was it busy or quiet?

Remind the children to listen carefully while others speak and to wait for their turn.

- Invite the children to draw two pictures. The first to show how they felt when they were ill and the second to show how they felt when they were better. Ask them to write two sentences to describe each picture.

- At the end of the session, invite some of the children to show their work to the others and to read out their sentences.

For Isabelle, William A, William G, George, Max, Emily,

Leo, Caspar, Felix, Tabitha, Phoebe, Harry and Libby –S.G.

Franklin Watts
This edition published in 2023 by
Hodder & Stoughton

Copyright © Hodder & Stoughton, 2023
All rights reserved.

Text © Hodder & Stoughton, 2023
Illustrations © Trevor Dunton 2021

The right of Trevor Dunton to be identified as the illustrator
of this Work has been asserted in accordance with the
Copyright, Designs and Patents Act, 1988.

Editor: Jackie Hamley
Designer: Cathryn Gilbert

A CIP catalogue record for this book is available
from the British Library.

ISBN 978 1 4451 7330 6 (hardback)
ISBN 978 1 4451 7331 3 (paperback)

Printed in China

Franklin Watts is a division of
Hachette Children's Books,
Part of Hodder & Stoughton
www.hachettechildrens.co.uk

MIX
Paper from
responsible sources
FSC
www.fsc.org
FSC® C104740